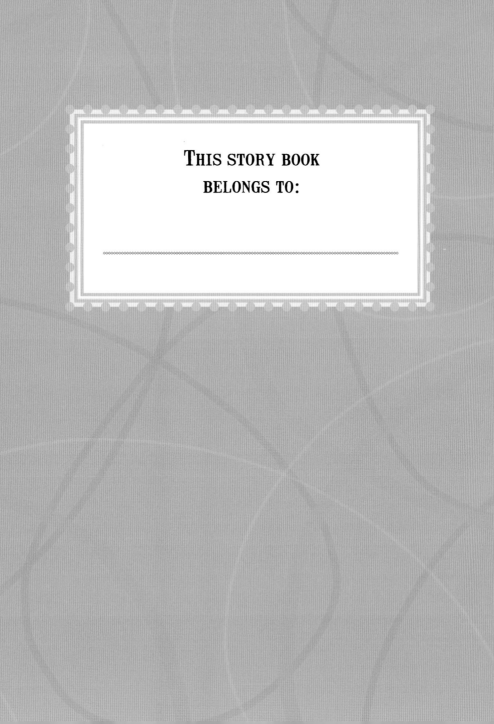

THIS STORY BOOK
BELONGS TO:

My First Storytime Treasury

A catalogue record for this book is available from the British Library

Published by Ladybird Books Ltd
80 Strand, London, WC2R 0RL
A Penguin Company

001
© LADYBIRD BOOKS LTD MMXII
LADYBIRD and the device of a Ladybird are trademarks of Ladybird Books Ltd

Each story previously published in Ladybird's 'My Storytime' series

ISBN: 978-0-72329-658-4

Printed in China

My First
Storytime
Treasury

~ Contents ~

THE TROUBLE WITH THOMAS TIGER

Every morning, all the jungle animals are woken up by Thomas Tiger's loud growl. But, one day, Thomas wakes up to find that his growl has gone. How will everyone in the jungle be woken up now?

SAM TRACTOR TO THE RESCUE

When a big storm closes in, Sam Tractor tries to get the farm animals to safety. But the animals won't listen to Sam Tractor!

LEWIS LION
LEARNS TO ROAR

*Lewis Lion hates lion lessons.
He prefers to laze around in the sun
all day. But, one night, Lewis hears a
rustling in the bushes. Will he remember
how to roar and pounce like a big lion?*

Page 67

DON'T WORRY
HENRY PUPPY

*Henry Puppy loves to visit
his best friend Sam Bunny,
but it's a long journey.
One day, little Henry loses his way!*

Page 93

SOPHIE SNAKE GETS IN A TWIST

Sophie Snake wakes up one morning with a knot in her slithery body. She tries sneezing it out and twirling it out, but it's no good. Will Sophie be stuck in a knot forever?

Page 119

ALFIE KITTEN MAKES A FRIEND

Alfie Kitten is the cheekiest little cat around. When a snooty new tabby comes to live in the neighbourhood, it's Alfie's job to cheer her up!

Page 145

HANNAH HIPPO'S NEW HELPER

All the hippos down by the muddy river have a special bird friend to eat the itchy insects that land on them. All except one! How will Hannah Hippo stop her itching and scratching?

Page 171

DAISY LEARNS TO DANCE

Daisy is nervous when she joins a new dance school. But there is a special place for her in the big show!

Page 197

THE TROUBLE WITH
THOMAS TIGER

written by Mandy Ross
illustrated by Jill McDonald

Every morning, as the sun rose over the jungle, Thomas Tiger would yawn and let out a huge growl!

GROWL!

Thomas's friends liked his morning
growl because it woke them up
before the sun got too hot.

Emma Elephant's breakfast grass was still soft and dewy. Hannah Hippo's mud was still nice and cool, and Gary Gorilla's favourite dozing spot was still leafy and shady – perfect!

But, one morning, as the sun rose over the jungle, Thomas woke up, yawned, and… nothing came out!

"Oh, no!" he whispered.
"I've lost my growl!"

With no special morning growl, everyone in the jungle slept late. By the time they got up, the sun was high in the sky.

Hannah's mud pool was boiling. Emma's grass was dry and hard. Gary's favourite dozing spot was hot and scratchy.

Everyone was miserable, especially Thomas.

"We've got to do something," said Emma. "If we don't help Thomas to get his growl back, we'll never wake up on time again."

"Let's play him some music," said Gary.
"Thomas might join in with a growl."

So Gary clapped some coconut shells together.
CLIPPETY-CLOP!

Hannah bubbled water.
BUBBLY-BOP!

And Emma drummed on a hollow tree trunk.
RUM-A-DUM-DUM!

CLIPPETY-CLOP!

Thomas opened his mouth to growl…
but nothing came out!

"It's no good," he said, "my growl
has gone."

Poor Thomas! He sadly tucked his
tail between his legs.

THUNK!

"Let's try to make him laugh," said Hannah. "That might bring his growl back."

She swung on a vine and crashed into a tree.

Gary slipped on a banana skin and fell into the mud pool.

SPLOSH!

Emma tripped over a log and landed on her bottom. It was all very silly.

SPLAT!

Thomas opened his mouth to growl
with laughter… but nothing came out!

"It's no good," he said, sadly. "I have to
get used to being growl-free."

And with that, he sloped off,
curled up tight and went to sleep.

Suddenly, Emma had an idea…

"I know just the thing to bring Thomas's growl back," she said. "Follow me."

She crept behind the rock where Thomas was sleeping.

"After three," said Emma. "Ready? One, two, *three*!"

They all jumped out with a super-loud
Trumpety-growly-gurgly-bellow!

Thomas nearly jumped out of his skin. He
got such a fright that he opened his mouth
and let out the most enormous growl!

"Hooray!" they all cheered.
"Thomas has found his growl!"

GRROWL!

From then on, nobody worried about sleeping late ever again. Their little growling alarm clock made sure of that!

GROWL!

SAM TRACTOR
TO THE RESCUE

written by Nicola Baxter

illustrated by Alex Burnett

Farmer Fred scratched his head. "It's going to snow and it's going to blow," he said, "or I'm a turnip. All the animals must come into the barn."

So Sam Tractor and his trailer trundled off across the farm to find the pigs.

The pigs were in the pen, snuffling and munching.

"You must come into the barn," said Sam Tractor.
"Farmer Fred thinks it's going to snow."

"Snow?" grunted the greedy pigs. "How does he know it's going to snow? We're staying right here… *snuffle*… with these… *munch*… tasty turnip tops, thank you very much." So off trundled Sam Tractor to find the cows.

The cows were in the meadow, chewing and mooing.

"You must come into the barn," said Sam Tractor. "Farmer Fred says it's going to snow."

"*Oooh, nooo,*" the cows mooed slowly. "A little bit of *snooow* doesn't worry us, you *knooow*. We're not… *chew*… leaving this… *chew*… *juuuicy* green grass, thank you very much." So off trundled Sam Tractor to find the hens.

The hens were in the yard, pecking and scratching.

"You must come into the barn," said Sam Tractor.
"Farmer Fred is sure it's going to snow."

"Snow? What's that?" clucked the hens nervously. "Now we're all of a twitter. Don't come bothering us… *cluck*… with silly… *cluck*… stories, thank you very much."

So off trundled Sam Tractor to find the ducks.

The ducks were in the pond, dipping and diving.

"You must come into the barn," said Sam Tractor.
"Farmer Fred is certain it's going to snow."

"Is that a fact?" quacked the dabbling ducks.
"We're not worried by a little bit of wind
and wet. We're... *quack*... happy... *quack*...
whatever the weather, thank you very much."

So off trundled Sam Tractor to find the sheep.

The sheep were on the hillside huddled together.

"You must come into the barn," said Sam Tractor. "Farmer Fred knows it's going to snow."

"The *baaarn*?" bleated the sheep.

"You must be *baaarmy*. Our woolly coats are the warmest on the *faaarm*, thank you very much."

So off trundled Sam Tractor to find the horse.

The horse was in the paddock, lazily leaning on the gate.

"You must come into the barn," said Sam Tractor. "Farmer Fred is as sure as he can be that it's going to snow."

"*Todaaay?*" neighed the horse with a yawn. "Oh, what a bore. I'd rather *staaay*, old chap, thank you very much."

So off trundled Sam Tractor back to the farmhouse.

Farmer Fred just stood and scratched his head again.

"If those uppity animals won't come," he said, "they can stay where they are. You can go into the barn."

He went back into the warm
farmhouse and banged the door shut.

As Sam Tractor trundled across
the yard, the first fluffy flakes of
snow began to fall.

Sam Tractor looked out from the barn. On the farm everything was white and whirling.

"It's snowing and blowing all right," he thought. "Oh bother! I can't stay here. I'm going to have to bring those uppity animals into the barn."

So off trundled Sam Tractor. The snow was cool and crunchy and icy wind whistled round his wheels.

Sam Tractor came to the pig pen. "Come on pigs, you can bring those turnip tops with you," he said. And the pigs climbed into the trailer without a grunt or a grumble.

Sam Tractor came to the meadow. "Come on cows, your grass isn't so green now!" he said. And the cows climbed into the trailer without a moo or a moan.

Sam Tractor came to the yard. "Come on hens, before your beaks turn blue!" he said. And the hens fluttered on board without a twitter or a cluck.

Sam Tractor came to the pond. It was
frozen solid. "Come on, you daft ducks,"
he said. And the ducks slid across the ice
without a single quack.

Sam Tractor came to the hillside.
Even the sheep were shivering.

"Come on, there's room for all of you,"
said Sam Tractor kindly. And they shuffled
on board without a baa or a bleat.

Sam Tractor came to the paddock.
"Come on horse, follow us!" he cried.
And the horse lolloped quietly behind
him all the way back to the barn.

All night long, it was snowing and blowing.
But Sam Tractor and the pigs and the cows
and the hens and the ducks and the sheep
and the horse were safe in the barn.

And with a *grunt* and a *moo* and a *cluck* and a *quack* and a *baa* and a *neigh*, all those uppity animals turned to say, "Sam Tractor, thank you very much!"

LEWIS LION
LEARNS TO ROAR

~

written by Ronne Randall
illustrated by Jill McDonald

Out on the sunny plain,
the Lion family lounged
and lazed. Lions love to laze!

Lewis Lion loved lazing more than
anyone. He loved to s-t-r-e-t-c-h
and feel the warm sun on his back…

and his belly…

and even his bottom!

71

Mum and Dad were teaching Lewis how to be a big lion. That meant learning to stalk, prowl and pounce.

"Show me what you've learned," said Mum.

STALK... PROWL... POUNCE!

went Lewis.

"Perfect!" said Mum.

73

Dad was teaching Lewis to growl, rumble and roar.

Lewis opened his mouth wide, and gave a mighty roar!

"Just right!" said Dad. "You'll soon be ready!"

ROARRR!

But, although Lewis was good at lion lessons,
his favourite time was when lessons were over.

Then he could snooze and snore in the sunshine.

Lewis's brother and sister always wanted to play.

"Get up!" said his sister.
"Let's play Leaping Lions!"

"Not now," said Lewis.
"I haven't finished napping yet!"

"Lewis!" called his brother.
"Let's chase butterflies!"

"Not now," said Lewis, turning over.
"I'm right in the middle of a
wonderful dream!"

"What a lazy lion you are!" said Mum.
"When you are a big lion, you will
have to stay awake for much longer."

"Then I want to stay a little lion
forever," said Lewis.
But he didn't really mean it.

Late one night, Lewis woke up suddenly. His nose began to twitch. Something was rustling nearby!

Lewis followed his nose into the bush.
He remembered what he'd learned in
lion lessons.

"I can be a big lion if I want to,"
he thought.

He STALKED...and PROWLED...

and he **POUNCED** with
a growl and a

ROARRR!

"Boo!" said Lewis's little sister.
"Ready to play Hide and Seek?"

"In the morning," yawned Lewis.
"It's time for sleep."

The next morning, while the other young lions were having lion lessons and playing, Lewis had a lie-in.

"Shhh," said Mum and Dad, when the other cubs tried to wake him. "Lewis needs his rest. He's a big lion now. A special roaring, prowling night-time lion!"

Lewis smiled, sleepily. Not only had he become a big lion, he could still spend all day doing just what he liked best… sleeping in the sun!

DON'T WORRY
HENRY PUPPY

~

written by Ronne Randall

illustrated by Simona Dimitri

Henry Puppy and Sam Bunny were best friends. Every day they played tag, chase-the-ball, who-can-jump-higher and hide-and-seek. They had so much fun together!

Then one day Sam moved away to a new home.
Henry was sad. He missed his friend.

But then Henry realised that he could go to visit Sam! As Sam's new home was far away, Henry made up a special rhyme to help him remember how to get there.

"Along the lane and past the mill,
Turn right at the big tree, go over the hill."

*"Past the field where the horses play —
I'm off to see Sam and I know the way!"*

Sam was always happy to see his friend. And Henry was happy to be there. But sometimes he felt a little worried.

"What if I forget the way next time I come?" he asked Sam. "Or what if I get lost going home?"

"You don't need to worry," Sam told him. "If you get lost, just go back the way you came! All you have to do is think of this special rhyme:

"If you lose your way,
Don't be downhearted.
Just follow your steps
Back to where you started!"

One night, there was a loud and blustery storm. The wind howled and moaned and shook the branches of the trees. Henry couldn't sleep.

"I hope I'll be able to visit Sam tomorrow," he thought.

By the next morning, the storm was over. The air was calm and clear, and the sun was shining.

"I will be able to visit Sam today," thought Henry happily.

As he set off, Henry noticed big heaps of leaves in the lane. "The storm must have blown them from the trees last night," he thought.

Henry jumped and danced through the leaves. "This is fun!" he laughed, kicking them high into the air.

As he went along, Henry said his rhyme to himself.

"*Along the lane and past the mill,*
Turn right at the big tree, go over the hill."

He ran along the lane as he always did, and scurried past the mill.

Suddenly Henry stopped. Where was the big tree? He couldn't see it anywhere! Henry was so confused that he didn't know which way to turn.

He ran down the lane, trying to remember the rest of the way to Sam's house.

"Past the fields where the horses play," he said to himself. *"I'm off to see Sam and I know the way!"*

But Henry didn't see the field where the friendly horses played. Instead he saw an old barn and some chickens.

"I can't remember seeing this on the way to Sam's house," he thought as he passed by.

Henry went on, and after a while he came to a field.

"This must be where the horses play!" he said to himself. But it wasn't. There were no horses in this field, just a raggedy old scarecrow.

"I can't remember seeing this on the way to Sam's house!" said Henry. He was very worried now. In fact, he felt like crying.

Then Henry remembered the rhyme Sam had taught him.

"If you lose your way,
Don't be downhearted.
Just follow your steps
Back to where you started!"

"That's what I need to do," thought Henry. "I'll go back the way I came!"

Back Henry went, past the scarecrow…
past the old barn…
and past the chickens.

At last Henry found himself back at the bottom of the hill.

"I know where I am now," he said. "And there's the big tree. It must have blown over in the storm last night!"

Henry leapt over the tree trunk, and scampered merrily down the lane. Before he knew it he could see his friends, the horses. *"Here's the field where the horses play,"* he said. *"I'm off to see Sam and I know the way!"*

And so little Henry found his way to Sam's home
at last.

"Oh, I'm so glad to see you!" Sam exclaimed. "I was
worried. I thought you might have got lost!"

"I did get lost," said Henry.
"Then how did you get here?" asked Sam.

"I did exactly what you told me to," said Henry. "Although I was lost, I wasn't downhearted – I just followed my steps back to where I started! And now I'll never worry about getting lost again!"

And off they went for a lively game of chase-the-ball.

SOPHIE SNAKE
GETS IN A TWIST

written by Melanie Joyce
illustrated by Jill McDonald

A ll through the jungle day, Sophie Snake wiggled and slithered happily around the jungle with her friends.

And every jungle night,
she curled herself into a
neat spiral to go to sleep.

But, one night, Sophie must have had very busy dreams. When she woke up in the morning, she had a big, fat knot in her tail.

"Oh no! Not a **KNOT**!" sighed Sophie.
She set off wiggling and slithering through the jungle.

But the knot kept getting caught between roots and branches. Every time, Sophie jumped and jerked and hurt herself.

"Oh, bad luck! Not a **KNOT**!"
said Sophie's friend, Thomas Tiger.
"When I've got a knot in my tail, I twirl
it round and round, and twirl it out."

So Sophie tried twirling her tail but, oh no! She found she couldn't twirl her tail on its own. Her whole body twirled round and round until she grew dizzy.

"And the knot's still there," she sighed.

Sophie met her friend Emma Elephant.

"Oh, bad luck! Not a **KNOT**!" she trumpeted. "When I've got a knot in my trunk, I go into the long tickly grass and try to sneeze it out."

Emma showed Sophie the
way to the long tickly grass.

AAA-CHOO!

Soon, they were both sneezing away.

"And the knot's still…
AAA-CHOO!"
sneezed Sophie.

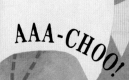

AAA-CHOO!

"I could just nip it out for you," offered
Carl Crocodile, with a glint of his teeth.

"No, thank you!" said Sophie,
slithering away as fast as she could.

"It's no good," she said, sadly. "I'm stuck with this knot forever and ever. I'll just have to get used to it."

But Sophie's friends hated
to see her so unhappy.

"If we can't untangle Sophie's knot, let's have a jungle dance. At least then we can try to cheer her up," they said.

139

That evening, all the animals gathered to dance to the jungle music. Sophie forgot the knot as she slithered and swirled and twisted and twirled with her dancing partners, until suddenly…

"My knot's gone!" she cried.
"Thank you, my friends!"

And then, under the jungle moon, Sophie
and her friends danced the night away.

ALFIE KITTEN
MAKES A FRIEND

written by Joan Stimson
illustrated by Simona Dimitri

Alfie Kitten was the cheekiest cat in the entire neighbourhood. He thought up the most brilliant games. He never ran out of jokes. And, when Alfie was around, it was almost impossible not to smile.

147

One day a new tabby kitten came to the neighbourhood. She was snooty and sniffy. She was vain and a pain. And right from the start she made it clear she was too busy worrying about her looks to enjoy herself.

"Don't take any notice," said Alfie's friends.

But Alfie couldn't bear to think of anyone not having fun. So the next day he bounded up to the new kitten with a cheerful, "Tabby Scowler, come and play. Try a smile and make my day!"

And then he began to tell his cheekiest puppy joke.

Alfie's friends laughed so loudly that he could hardly hear himself speak. Tabby thought the joke was funny too. But then she remembered: "I've just arranged my whiskers. If I have a good laugh, they'll get in a tangle again."

So, instead of joining in, Tabby simply scowled some more. And stuck her nose in the air.

Alfie was disappointed. But the next day he bounded up to the new kitten with a cheerful, "Tabby Scowler, come and play. Try a smile and make my day!"

And then he began to describe his latest game. "It's called Run, Wriggle and Roll," said Alfie.

His friends were already purring expectantly.
But Tabby looked confused. So Alfie explained.
"Run around the garden, wriggle through the
hedge and roll down the bank." *Whoooosh!*
The other kittens all rushed off together.

For a moment Tabby was caught up in the excitement too. But, as the other kittens disappeared into the hedge, she remembered: "I've just washed my fur. And, if I wriggle and roll, it will get all messy again."

So, instead of joining in, Tabby simply scowled some more. And stuck her nose in the air.

Alfie was shocked. But that evening he bounded up to the new kitten with a cheerful, "Tabby Scowler, come and play. Try a smile and make my day!"

And then he began to set up his moonlight shadow show. His friends were already practising bending and twisting by the wall.

Tabby thought perhaps she could make an exciting shadow shape too. But then she remembered: "I've just draped myself elegantly over the wall. And, if I twist my tail into a snake, I might not be able to make it elegant again."

So, instead of joining in, Tabby simply scowled some more. And stuck her nose in the air.

Alfie was beside himself.

"Don't give her a second thought," said all his friends. But Alfie was determined.

"I'll make that kitten enjoy herself," he announced, "if it's the last thing I do."

The next day Alfie waited patiently for his chance.
And that afternoon he crept up to the new kitten…
in total silence. The sun was warm. And Tabby was
taking a cat nap.

"If I can just find her tickle spot," thought Alfie to
himself, "then she's bound to burst out…"

"How dare you disturb my beauty sleep!" roared Tabby. And suddenly she was wide awake and furious!

Tabby chased Alfie right round the garden. She leapt after him as he dived for the safety of the hedge. And, when Alfie rolled head over paws down the bank, Tabby somersaulted after him.

By the time she caught up with Alfie,
Tabby was a changed kitten.

"He's gone too far this time," groaned all Alfie's
friends.

"Shall I help you re-arrange your whiskers?"
asked Alfie.

"No!" bellowed Tabby. "I'm enjoying myself far too much to worry about my whiskers," she explained. "And after that amazing chase, I'm in the mood for a good joke!"

"Now," she nudged Alfie. "Have you heard the one about the puppy from Peru?"

Alfie shook his head in astonishment.

"Well," went on the new kitten,
"*There once was a puppy I knew,*
Who lived on the plains of Peru.
He wasn't too bright,
But he danced every night
As he dined upon dinosaur stew!"

Then she rolled around the grass in hysterics.

It made Alfie's day to see Tabby enjoying herself.

And, from then on, whenever he thought up a new game, Alfie could be sure that Tabby Smiler would be the first to join in!

HANNAH HIPPO'S
NEW HELPER

written by Ronne Randall
illustrated by Jill McDonald

Deep in the jungle, there was
a winding, wandering river.
It was the glubbiest, blubbiest,
muddiest river anywhere.
Perfect for hippos!

173

Hannah Hippo and her friends *loved* the mud! They played games like...

KICK SPLASH...

MUD PADDLE...

AND EVEN DEEP-MUD DIVING!

No matter how hot and steamy the jungle
was, the mud was always nice and cool.

In fact, the only things that ever made the hippos hot were the buzzing, nipping insects that flew around the river.

Luckily for the hippos, the friendly birds who lived around the river thought the insects were delicious. Each bird chose its favourite hippo and sat on its back quietly feasting on bugs and flies.

So most of the hippos were very happy. All except one.

Poor Hannah didn't have her own
bird friend to eat up all the bugs!

"This buzzing and biting and itching and
twitching is driving me mad!" said Hannah.
"I'll have to find a friend of my own!"

181

So Hannah set off up the river.

Soon, she met Carl Crocodile. "Hello, Hannah,"
said Carl Crocodile, snapping his shiny white teeth.
"I'll help you to get rid of those biting bugs!"

"No, thanks," said Hannah,
swimming past as fast as she could.

Hannah swam further up the river.

"Hello, Hannah!" shouted Lewis Lion and Thomas Tiger. "We'll help you to swish those nasty flies away with our tails!"

"No, thanks," said Hannah,
swimming quickly by.
"That won't work for me!"

Soon, Hannah was in a part of the jungle she'd never seen before. She was a little bit scared.

"Maybe I'd better go home, before I get lost," she thought.

But, suddenly, Hannah heard something in the trees. It was a little bird.

Hannah waved to the bird, and the bird fluttered down and settled on her tummy. The bird picked and pecked hungrily, and soon all the bugs were gone!

Before long, Hannah was swimming happily
home with her new friend on her back.

"No more itching or twitching!" thought Hannah.
"Thank you, Little Bird!"
"TWEET!" cheeped Little Bird.

"Welcome home, Hannah!" called her friends. "We thought you were lost. Where have you been?"

"I've been all the way up the river," said Hannah. "And I've found a new friend."

"TWEET!" said Little Bird.

Hannah knew what that meant…

She had her own special bird friend at last.
And no more itches!

195

DAISY
LEARNS TO DANCE

written by Marie Birkinshaw

illustrated by Simona Dimitri

Daisy loved to dance. More than anything else, she wanted to be a famous ballet dancer. Every night she dreamed of performing in front of a real audience.

Today was Daisy's first lesson at her new dancing school. As she walked into the huge hall, she felt a bit worried.

"Hello Daisy," said Mrs Pringle, the dancing teacher. Daisy thought Mrs Pringle looked beautiful – elegant, tall and graceful.

Then Daisy met the rest of the class. They had all been to the ballet school before. Daisy was the only new one there and she was by far the smallest dancer in the hall. Now she began to feel very worried indeed.

Daisy looked around at the other dancers. They were warming up, ready for the lesson to begin.

She could see Selina and Sophie, admiring themselves in the mirror. They were so tall and slender. Then there was a group of dancers exercising at the barre.

Suddenly, three boys came rushing across the room and knocked Daisy over. They were the Noisy Trio, as Mrs Pringle called them – Jack, Dan and Andrew.

"Whoops! Sorry!" Jack said to Daisy. "You're so small, we didn't see you."

"Listen now, everyone!" called Mrs Pringle. "This summer I would like the class to perform *The Silver Swan*, and you will all take part."

Everyone cheered. They had all heard of *The Silver Swan*. The costumes were great, and the music was brilliant with lots of drums, trumpets and tinkling chimes.

Daisy wasn't sure what it was, but she felt excited all the same.

"This morning," said Mrs Pringle, "I am going to choose who will play each part. We will start with the trees. Listen to the music and watch carefully!"

Mrs Pringle waved her arms and danced on the spot. She looked just like a beautiful tree swaying in the breeze.

Swish!

'Swish!

Swish!
Swish!

"Now it's your turn!" said Mrs Pringle.

The dancers waved their arms and danced on the spot.

Swish! Swish! Swish! Swish!

Mrs Pringle chose Selina and Sophie to be the trees... but she didn't choose Daisy.

"Next," said Mrs Pringle, "I want you to dance like fire! Listen to the music and watch carefully."

Mrs Pringle danced towards Selina and Sophie. Her arms leapt out, like fiery flames around slender trees.

FLICKER!

FLICKER!

CRACKLE!

CRACKLE!

"Now it's your turn!" said Mrs Pringle.

The dancers leapt round the hall like raging fire.

FLICKER! FLICKER! CRACKLE! CRACKLE!

"Very good!" said Mrs Pringle, and she chose the Noisy Trio to be the flames…
but she didn't choose Daisy.

"Now," called Mrs Pringle, tapping her stick for attention, "I want you to pretend to be woodland creatures, running away from the flames. Listen to the music and watch carefully."

Mrs Pringle ran away from the Noisy Trio like a frightened animal. SWOOSH! SWOOSH! SCAMPER! SCAMPER!

"Now it's your turn!" she said. Everyone danced their very best.

Swoosh! Swoosh! Scamper! Scamper!

Mrs Pringle chose the rest of the dancers to be the woodland creatures…
but she didn't choose Daisy.

Daisy was the only dancer without a part.
She wanted to cry.

"Now," said Mrs Pringle, "I would usually choose
an older dancer for the star role, but this year I have
decided to do something a little different. The Silver
Swan will fly across the stage on dancers' ropes.
For this we need the smallest and lightest dancer
in the school."

Everyone looked at Daisy.

"I know this is your very first lesson, Daisy," Mrs Pringle said, "but I wonder if you would like to be the Silver Swan?"

Daisy was thrilled. "Me?" she gasped. "Oh, Mrs Pringle, I'd love to!"

So the ropes were tied round Daisy's waist, and she swept across the stage.

Daisy's class practised really hard that summer. At the end of term, they put on their special performance of *The Silver Swan*. Everyone came to see it.

The curtain rose and the musicians began to play.

SWISH! SWISH! SWISH! SWISH!

The trees swayed in the breeze. But then the wind grew stronger and stronger.

Suddenly there was a loud crack, as lightning struck the trees and flames leapt around them.

FLICKER! FLICKER! CRACKLE! CRACKLE!

The woodland creatures started to flee.

Swoosh! Swoosh! Scamper! Scamper!

They were terrified and didn't know where to go. Just then the animals looked up. There above them, swooping softly and silently was the Silver Swan. She would lead them to safety.

And Daisy, the little dancer, glided gently before them and led the woodland creatures safely to the Silver Lagoon.

Everyone clapped and cheered and shouted for more.

The musicians and dancers had done so well that Mrs Pringle wanted to cry for joy.

Daisy was the proudest little dancer in the whole ballet school. Perhaps one day she would be famous, after all!